D1564222

CHINESE CLASSICS

THE PEONY PAVILION

Tang Xianzu

Retold by Teng Jianmin

CHINA INTERCONTINENTAL PRESS

图书在版编目（CIP）数据

牡丹亭故事：英文 / 滕建民改编；顾伟光，(美) 马洛甫 (Marloff, S.) 译. -- 北京：五洲传播出版社，2011.8
ISBN 978-7-5085-2161-9

Ⅰ. ①牡… Ⅱ. ①滕… ②顾… ③马… Ⅲ. ①传奇剧（戏曲）-剧本-中国-明代-英文 Ⅳ. ①I237.2

中国版本图书馆CIP数据核字(2011)第152766号

改　　编：滕建民
英文翻译：顾伟光，(美) 马洛甫 (Marloff, S.)

策划编辑：荆孝敏
责任编辑：郑　磊
设计总监：闫志杰
封面设计：叶　影
设计制作：蔡育朋

出版发行：五洲传播出版社
地　　址：北京市海淀区北三环中路31号生产力大楼B座7层
邮　　编：100088
网　　址：www.cicc.org.cn
电　　话：010-82005927，010-82007837
印　　刷：北京冶金大业印刷有限公司
开　　本：889×1194mm　1/32
印　　张：3.25
版　　次：2012年1月第1版　2012年1月第1次印刷
定　　价：68.00元

Contents

CHAPTER I

The story happened in the Southern Song Dynasty (1127-1279) that covers regions south of the Yangtze River after the fall of the Northern Song Dynasty. With its capital in Lin'an (now Hangzhou, Zhejiang Province) and nine emperors reigning for 153 years, this dynasty was economically strong, technologically developed and more accessible to the outside world. However, its military was weak and its leaders incompetent. Since its establishment, the Southern Song had been under the constant threat of the Jin Dynasty (1157-1234) which was founded by the Jurchens in Manchuria in the northeastern part of China.

Du Bao, the magistrate of Nan'an Prefecture, Jiangxi province and his wife had a baby daughter, their only child. They named her Du Liniang. The girl grew into an intelligent beauty. In the daddy's mind, the daughter is a smart girl from an eminent family and she should have a good knowledge of Chinese classics beyond needlework. Only in this way could she communicate better with a young scholar when the time came for her to marry him. Furthermore, they would feel greatly honored if their daughter is regarded as being well-educated and reasonable by her husband's family. So, having consulted with his wife, the magistrate planned to hire a tutor for their daughter.

Having heard the news, young scholars rushed to the girl's house one after another for interviews but the father didn't feel comfortable with any of the applicants. He did not want to see those young lads whirling round his beautiful daughter who's coming of marriageable age, fearing that should anything unexpected happens, it would not only hurt his daughter's reputation but also his family's fame. So her would- be tutor has to be experienced and prudent. Having turned down all the young male applicants, he eventually hired Chen Zuiliang, an old scholar in his late 50'.

Son of a doctor, the man had been a talented boy raised in the traditional Confucianism, who had read through the Chinese classics, could write beautiful essays and passed the imperial examination at county level at age 12. But his luck stopped here. No matter how hard he studied, his good luck never came back. He had taken totally 15 examinations at provincial level, once in every 3 years but he had failed them all. 40 some years passed, he had never earned any scholarly official rank. He inherited a drugstore from his father, surviving on the small sum of money that brought in. The younger scholars mocked this ill-fated old man and nicknamed him Chen, the No-food. Since he knew a little about medicine, augury and geomancy, he was also called Chen, the Knowledgeable. Another round of county-level examination was approaching, but he really felt that he was getting too old to pass it for this time, so he decided against taking it. When he heard that the magistrate wanted to hire a tutor he decided to join the crowd for fun without any expectation. Unexpectedly, this old and pedantic scholar was indeed selected by the Du family for two simple reasons. First of all, this old scholar was knowledgeable enough to teach his daughter, and secondly, since Du had only one child and felt lonely all the time, he hoped that this scholar could spare some time chitchatting or playing chess with him after his daughter's class.

Now that the tutor has been selected, coming next will be choosing a lucky day for the daughter to pay her respect to her tutor. On that occasion, the tutor will be told that Chunxiang (literally Spring Fragrance), the private servant girl will accompany the daughter to study.

"My daughter is all my pride and joy. I love her very much. As I have no son, I raised her like a boy", Du told the scholar.

"She is a smart girl and has already read through quite a few classics from my family library, including the Four Books (The Great Learning, The Doctrine of the Mean, The Analects of Confucius and The Words of Mencius), I would suggest that you teach her the Five Classics (The Book of Songs, The Book of History, The Book of Changes, The Book of Rites and The Spring and Autumn Annals), since the Book of Changes is about yin, yang and the Eight Diagrams which are too abstruse to understand, and the Book of History is about managing state affairs, which is unrelated to a girl's life. Same is true about the Book of Rites and the Spring and Autumn Annals. Why don't you start from the Book of Songs and teach her the poems with rhyme and stories about the virtues of the queen and concubines, as part of her orthodox education? Chen was also informed that Chunxiang would accompany Liniang in her classes.

The old scholar dared not to neglect the satrap's request and also felt it reasonable. To start with, he decided to teach the girl a poem selected from the Book of Songs as per the request of the magistrate.

One beautiful spring day, after he washed and had breakfast, the tutor sat up in the study waiting for the girl to come to his class. After several hours, his back began to ache and still nobody showed up. The tutor could not help but lament with sighs about the spoiled girl. He got so impatient and annoyed that he sent the maid to fetch Liniang.

The girl did not want any tutor and was frustrated with the old-fashioned teaching. When her maid came to tell her that the tutor was waiting, she reluctantly went with her to the study session.

Having received the girl's curtsey, the old tutor told the Liniang that a girl should get up before dawn and pay respect to

her parents tight after she washes and dresses up. After sunrise, she should do things she is told to do. Now you are supposed to study in class, so you must get up early and come to class on time.

Knowing she is in the wrong, she said tamely to the tutor that she would never be late.

"We understand," the maid chimed in. "We will not go to sleep tonight. Why don't you come to teach us at midnight?"

The old tutor glared at the maid, opened the Book of Songs and began his teachings in sad earnest.

Chunxiang was a naughty and playful little girl of only 14 or 15 years old. Accompanying the young lady of the family to learn is like putting her in shackles. How could she possibly sit still and keep quiet? So, she would butt in occasionally while the old tutor taught.

The poem the old tutor decided to teach first was one in the Book of Songs.

Ospreys are chirping for love at the shoal, and
Slim and beautiful ladies are good partners for gentlemen

He explained to the young lady that the osprey in the poem is a type of bird with beautiful songs.

"What do they sound like?" asked the maid.

To the girls' surprise, the old tutor began chirping like an osprey. Chunxiang couldn't help but began imitating him.

Ignoring her, the old tutor continued to explain that ospreys are relatively quiet birds that live on the shoal.

"Right", the main interrupted again. "There was a turtle dove in our mansion this year or last, I am not too sure. The young lady master set it free and it flew to the State Governor's house."[1]

[1]The words "Shoal" and "State Governor' are homophones.

"Nonsense", irritated by the maid's constant interruptions, the old tutor said angrily. "This is simply a qixing in the poem, a stimulant that inspire poet's train of thoughts".

"What's a qixing, again?" the maid asked.

"It's something that inspires the verses that follows. In this case, the sentence 'the slim and beautiful ladies are good partners for gentlemen' implies that a quiet and docile lady will be courted by a gentleman. Chen answered her question but, trying to avoid the subject of courting men and women, he said it with a deliberate equivocation.

"Why does the gentleman court her?" The piquant maid probed.

"You ask too many questions". Chen scolded, his face growing red.

"Teacher, we can try to understand the annotations of the verse by themselves. Why don't you tell us more about the general ideas of the poem," Du Liniang hurriedly interjected, trying to ease the tension.

At that, the old tutor solemnly started his teaching. This is in fact a popular love poem which has been extorted by many literati to the works that praises the virtues of the concubines in the royal court. The old tutor would naturally explain the meanings of the poem from the orthodox viewpoint, from the virtuous and open-minded ladies to their appearance and bearing. All the old-fashioned moralizations!

When the class was over, Du Liniang became sleepy. After the truism, the old tutor asked her to practice calligraphy. He got upset when he found that the writing brushes, ink sticks, paper and ink stones which he sent the maid to fetch were not right. However, he was greatly impressed by Du Liniang's handwritings. How can such a gentle and frail-looking girl handwrite such beautiful characters?

While Du Liniang practiced calligraphy under her tutor's guidance, the maid slipped away. Unaware of the time passed, Miss Du wanted her maid back but couldn't find her. Still puzzled, she saw her maid running into the room, breathing heavily.

Only at this moment was the old tutor aware of the maid's absence, so he asked her angrily: "where have you been, you little girl?"

"There's a garden out there with a wide variety of flowers and grass," the maid told her mistress, completely ignoring the tutor. "That's a nice place to play."

"How could you go to that garden instead of reading your books?" scolded the old tutor. "Wait till I bring my whipping twigs."

"What are your whipping twigs for?" asked the maid boldly. Seeing the stupefied old man standing there, she said, "We girls don't take the imperial exams and we don't take government posts. All we're doing here is to learn to read. What's the big deal?"

"Do you know about a scholar named Che Yin," asked the tutor in attempt to reason with the maid. "He was too poor to buy oil for his reading lamp that he put the fireflies into a bag to light up the room for reading. Another poor scholar named Jiang Mi would read even by moonlight.

"Enough," the maid retorted. "Reading by moonlight hurts eyes and it's so cruel to put the fireflies into a bag."

"Years ago, there were people who studied so assiduously and tirelessly that they would tie their hair on the beams of the reading room or prick their thigh with an awl to keep awake."

"That's even more outrageous, tying hair on the beams would certainly hurt their hair and pricking thigh with awls would leave scars. This is not something to brag about."

Their argument was interrupted by the calls of a street vendor selling flowers outside. The maid told Miss Du, you hear the flower peddler's call on the street? Doesn't that sound much like more fun than the school work in here?"

"You are misleading the young mistress. Now I really must beat you." With that he got up, raised the twig and beat her. The maid was hiding behind the young mistress. He missed, raising his arm to try again but the maid grabbed his twig from his hand and threw it to the ground.

The old tutor's face grew white with anger. Liniang quickly interjected and asked the maid to apologize to the old man.

"You stupid girl. How dare you to offend the tutor like so?" Realizing how angry she had made her mistress, Chunxiang

knelt down on the ground tamely. The young mistress turned to the tutor and begged, "Teacher, this girl is young and foolish. Since this is her first wrongdoing, please give her a chance and spare her physical punishment. She won't play in that garden again".

Chunxiang, however, didn't realize that Liniang was simply trying to calm down her tutor.

"Oh you don't think I would dare to go back there. Let's just wait and see", she talked back to the young mistress.

The young mistress said she would report her maid's behavior to her mother, the lady of the family for punishment. She winked at her maid who immediately understood what Liniang was up to.

"Please forgive me, Young Mistress and Tutor. I will never do that again".

Seeing that the young mistress was so persistent, the tutor sighed and said "Forget it. I'll let it go this time. Now get up."

Chen gave Liniang her assignment and told her she could

only leave when the work was finished. He then left the two girls and went to have chitchat with Liniang's father.

"He is so pedantic and foolish," complained the maid once the tutor was gone. "He has no idea how to enjoy life."

"Don't act so ignorant and think he can't punish you," Liniang scolded her. "Just as the proverb says, he who teaches you for one day becomes your father for life. Now come over and tell me where that garden is."

The maid glared at the young mistress, and turned her back ignoring her. Liniang smiled. She moved closer and pleaded "Good girl. Please tell me."

"Just over there," Chunxiang pointed out the window towards the garden.

All Liniang could see was a thick shadow of trees. "What's behind those trees?"

"There's so much to see! At least six or seven pavilions, swings, grotesque rocks from Taihu Lake, a stream surrounded by lots of exotic flowers and grass. It's beautiful!"

"I never expected there would be such a nice place", the young mistress muttered to herself. Her heart has long been to the vibrant garden.

CHAPTER II

To outsiders Du Liniang is a talented, beautiful and intelligent girl from a respectable family. Like others this carefree girl had her own set of problems. Her father was from an old-fashioned aristocratic family with high prestige in the locality. A family like his was definitely not liberal. He would ask his daughter not to walk out of the house by herself and not to show her teeth when she smiled. As she grew older, she became prettier like a flower. However, the father pinched the bud tightly in his hand before the delicate and charming flower blooms. Under such rigid and rigorous home education and control, much of Miss Du's natural instinct has been inhibited. She became more and more dignified and modest, showing demeanor of a prestigious family when she behaved. All in all, the dull and tedious atmosphere of the grand mansion made her feel unhappy. Having read the verse "Ospreys are chirping for love at the shoal, and slim and beautiful ladies are good partners for gentlemen" in the Book of Songs, she became volatile and her heart restless. She was often distracted and felt ill at ease when she read books in class. She would put down her books and kept on sighing.

One day, when the maid noticed how unhappy the young mistress appeared she encouraged her to go play in the garden. The young mistress certainly wanted to go but she was afraid of her parents' rebuke and scold. "The master has gone to inspect the crops in the countryside and won't be back for days." the maid told her. "What are you afraid of?"

The young mistress hesitated briefly and, unable to resist the temptation, plucked up her courage and went with the maid to explore the garden.

Beyond the gate was gorgeous scenery of spring. The green buds are sprouting. The red, white, yellow and pink flowers were blooming so bright and shining that Liniang gasped. The garden

made her happy. Coming out of the inanimate boudoir and into a surrounding of beautiful flowers, she suddenly felt relieved. Everything before her eyes was so pleasing to see. She wondered why her dad had never taken her to the garden, not even mentioned the existence of it.

Together the girls wandered through the garden, came around the rockery, through the wisteria pergola, stopped by the peony railing to watch the flying butterflies over the flowers and listen the yellow warbler singing at the Peony Pavilion. The beauty and vitality of the garden intoxicated her completely.

Seeing that such vibrant and beautiful scenery is locked up behind the wall and fell into disuse, suggestive of the circumstance she was in, the young mistress was a bit sentimental. She was like the flowers in the garden, beautiful but unknown, locked up behind the walls of the mansion. The beautiful peony would wither and fall after the spring season and eventually only the dead twigs and withered leaves remained. The young mistress thought to herself that she might shares the same destiny with those falling peonies. Disturbed by the thought, she sighed and quickly lost the excitement over and interest in the beautiful scenery before her eyes.

"Chunxiang, I'm tired. Let's leave here."

When Liniang returned to her boudoir she threw herself onto her bed. She felt tired from the walk in the garden and fell asleep over the table.

She dreamed that a young scholar, holding a willow twig in his hand, entered her room.

"Young mistress, I have been looking for you and here you are," he spoke softly.

Liniang stood up quickly, puzzled and shocked. She had never spoken to any young man before and therefore could not think of anything to say. Speechless, she gave him a quick glance, her head spinning.

"I plucked a willow twig when I passed through the garden", the young man said. "You are such a talented girl. Could you compose a poem praising the willow tree?"

Though she didn't know him, he gave her an impression of a refined and learned person. And he was handsome. Yet she was confused. "How did he know me if we have never met before," She asked herself. She wanted to talk to the young man but knew that girls, especially ones of her status, weren't supposed to do such things. He seemed to have read her mind.

"Young mistress, it's so beautiful out. How about a walk in the garden," said the young man, holding her hand in his.

They walked into the garden together. She felt as if he was walking her into a fairyland. He softly whispered his love into her ear and she bashfully listened in silence. She felt the spring scenery in the garden was getting more gorgeous and flirtatious. All the flowers seemed to smile toward her and birds ceaselessly sing their songs. Surrounded by the beautiful peonies, the congenial pair holds each other tightly beside the Peony Pavilion. The girl had the warm and sweet feeling she never felt before. She closed her eyes and enjoyed to the greatest extend the fascination and emotional attachment.

Nobody knew how long they sat there before she heard the nameless young man said, "Young mistress, you must be tired. Let me escort you back." The young man accompanied her back to her boudoir and said, "I must go now. Sweet dreams."

She didn't want him to leave and was about to walk him to the door when her mother burst into the room. Her eyes flew open, only to realize there was no one else in the room. It had all been a dream. Her face fell. Dreams were illusory, but this one was sweat and evocative. She felt even more alone than before.

CHAPTER III

Ever since she dreamed about seeing the young scholar with willow twig in hand, the young mistress couldn't help but immersing in her dreamland, unable to extricate herself. She couldn't get the young man and the time they spent at the Peony Pavilion out of her mind. Gradually, she became so depressed and disconnected from her life that she didn't feel like eating and sleeping.

The maid began to worry about her mistress. As Liniang grew thinner, Chunxiang confronted her.

"Ever since we returned from the garden that day, you seemed to have lost your appetite. You have lost so much weight. If it goes on like this, I'm afraid you may lose much of your beauty, too."

Completely unaware of her weight loss, the young mistress was taken aback by the word. She rushed to the mirror to see for herself and was startled by the frail image of the girl she saw looking back at her.

"I was such a beauty, coquettish and exquisite, and have never expected I would look so haggard," the young mistress sighed. "I must hurry and have my portrait painted now or no one will ever know how pretty I once was."

With that she asked Chunxiang to bring her silk scroll, ink and brush pen. When the maid brought these items Liniang began to paint her own portrait out of the reflection in the mirror. She showed the finished work to the maid who gasped in admiration. "You are so talented! The picture looks so real, just like your shadow. But there's one thing missing."

"What is it?" asked the young mistress.

"There ought to be a young man beside you. If you marry to a fine husband and a portrait of you two would be hanging on the wall. Wouldn't that be great?"

At this, the young mistress smiled. "Can I tell you a secret? Without waiting for an answer, she rushed on. "I met someone in the garden last time I was there."

"What? How? I didn't see anyone".

"I met him in my dream".

"How did he look like?"

"He was a young scholar with a willow twig in his hand," the young mistress told her maid. "He asked me to compose a poem. Maybe that means the man I am going to marry has anything to do with the willow tree and is surnamed Liu (a homonym for "willow" in Chinese)?" I didn't even have a chance to talk to him, not even responded when he asked me about the poem. What if I write a poem and put it on the portrait of me?"

"That's a great idea," agreed the maid.

She pondered for a while then started to write a poem over the portrait.

She is a dignified lady if seen from nearby and a dancing fairy from afar.

If you want to meet this goddess of the moon, she can be found by the willow or close to the plum.

After she completed her poem, the young mistress drew a slender and graceful willow tree behind her. She put down the brush pen and sighed.

"For centuries women either got married early and had their portraits painted by their husbands, or the painted self-portrait and gave them to their lovers," Miss Du said sadly. "I have painted my self-portrait and inscribed a on it but who should I give the painting to?" At this she started to cry.

The following morning she awoke terribly sick. After several

days and no sign of recovery, her mother went to the maid and asked her what had happened. Chunxiang told her everything including the walk through the garden and Liniang's dream. The old lady was shocked and believed that a ghost had bewitched her daughter. The lord was furious when he heard this.

"I hired a tutor to teach and restrain your daughter. How could you have allowed her to run around like so? As the mother, you are to blame for failing to properly discipline your daughter."

"You're not blaming me for this. She is old enough to be married and I've wanted to find her a husband for some time now. If she'd been married she would have never gotten sick like this."

"Our daughter is too young to get married now. The most important thing for her is to become well-educated and reasonable. It's too early to her to know about sex. I don't think our daughter is seriously sick. I have sent someone for Old Chen who has studied medicine to make a diagnosis. She will be alright once he prescribes something for her."

"How do you know she wasn't bewitched by a sprite or pixie in the garden," Mrs. Du argued. "If this is the case then medicine won't work. In my opinion, we'd need a Taoist nun to eliminate evil sprites and dispel misfortunes by conducting religious rites."

"A sprite or a pixy? Nonsense," the lord exclaimed. "That's the view of a superstitious woman. Now that she is sick, she must see the physician."

They argued back and forth for some time, but eventually he ordered his wife to make arrangements for the doctor to come. Though she was obligated to do as her husband asked, she decided to invite a nun, nicknamed Mother Stone to the house as well.

The physician came. He diagnosed by feeling her pulse and had a small chat with the girl but still couldn't find the cause of her illness. He prescribed her some medicine to get rid of the pathogenic heat and then left. The nun came next. She burned paper with "magic" characters written on it and chanted incantations but nothing seemed to work. When the rite was over, Miss Du seemed to be sicker than before.

Time passed. The Mid-Autumn Festival has arrived and Liniang was still confined to her sickbed. The window was open so she could hear the wind outside and feel the chill in the air.

"It is getting cold and the moon seems bright. W hat's the date today," she asked her maid, struggling to sit up.

"August 15."

"It's the Mid-Autumn Day." This house is cold and cheerless and there is no sign of festivity. My parents are in no mood to admire the full moon tonight. Help me up to the window. I want to see the moon."

With the help of her maid, Miss Du managed to reach the window. It was completely dark and the moon looked exceptionally bright. The moonlight shone on the ground liked as if it was covered by snow. To Liniang the beautiful night view was nothing but desolation. She thought of the lonely Goddess in the Moon Palace and of her own destiny. Alone and sick, she felt lonelier than ever before and knew that her days were numbered. She asked her maid to put her self-portrait in a sandalwood case and hide it underneath the rockery in the back garden. A gust of wind swept through the air, Miss Du could hear the sound of dying insects in the grass and of leaves falling from trees. She couldn't help but think that this was an omen from heaven about her fate. She quailed and fainted at the window.

The maid, frightened for her young mistress, hurriedly helped her to the bed and sent for her mother. The Madame rushed to her daughter's room, saw Liniang's pale face and felt her cold feet, she wailed. After some time, the young mistress awoke to her mother sitting beside her bed and crying.

"Mom, I'm sorry. I can no longer serve you but in my next existence I will do better."

"My child, stop thinking like that." When the old lady finally managed to get control of her tears she tried to comfort her daughter. "Get some rest and everything's going to be alright."

"Mom, I know I am dying but I have a request of you." "Go ahead and speak your mind."

"There is a plum tree in the garden. I love it dearly. I hope to be buried behind it after my death."

Her mother's heart broke. Holding her daughter tightly, she lost control and cried so hard she almost passed out. The maid worried for both of them and rushed to get the lord. W hen he came, the young mistress was at her last gasp. When the old man saw his only daughter dying like this, he cried uncontrollably and his face covered with tears.

The young mistress died the very night.

Her parents were terribly sad over the loss of their daughter. The entire household mourned the girl's death.

While the household was in great grief, the Jin army intruded the southern part of the country and the emperor sent out an order for the lord to act as the garrison commander of Yangzhou, a bigger area than his hometown. He was ordered to proceed to his new post immediately. Mr. Du intended to leave without delay. Liniang was buried underneath the plum tree beside the rockeries in the garden as she wished.

He left the tutor Chen and the nun Mother Stone in charge of building a Plum Blossom Nunnery in the garden, in which the young mistress was consecrated. He asked the abbess to preside over the nunnery and attend to the sacrifices and tutor to watch over their daughter's grave. With everything was arranged, Mr. Du left with his wife and their entourage to go to his new post.

CHAPTER IV

Coincidently, there was a handsome scholar named Liu Sheng of whom the young mistress had dreamed. The young man came from a poor family in Lingnan and was now just over 20. Talented and hardworking, he has passed the imperial examination at the provincial level but hadn't been able to continue on to become a jinshi, the successful candidate in the highest imperial examinations to be held in the capital. Not long ago, he dreamed of meeting a pretty girl under a plum tree in a beautiful garden. He heard her say: "Liu, you will not have a happy marriage and be successful in career without me". He tried many times but still could not shake off the memory of the dream. He hoped it would bring him good luck. When he woke up, he changed his name to Liu Mengmei, literally, dreaming the plum, to commemorate their encounter.

Though Liu was well educated, he was nearly broke and could barely make ends meet by the income from a hunchbacked ser vant planting fruit trees. In hopes of something better, he went to his friend Han Zicai for advice. Han recommended Miao Shunbin, an imperial envoy. Miao has a deep appreciation and love for talents. He was also a connoisseur of the imperial court.

Guangzhou (Canton) was a trading port between the Song Dynasty and Southeast Asian countries and a depot for rare jewels and precious stones. Though Jin repeatedly invaded and harassed the land up in the north, the Song emperor still indulged himself with all sorts of wants. He would send his envoys to collect rare treasures. This was exactly Miao's job. A big fair would be held every three years in Guangzhou where jewelers from the Southeast Asian countries would come and display their treasures. Han advised Liu to take the opportunity and meet Miao at the fair. He promised Liu that his talents would surely be recognized by the emperor's envoy. Liu took his advice, packed up his belongs and left for the fair.

When he arrived at the temple where the fair was held, he begged for a meeting with Miao. The monk guarding the gate notified the official inside that a juren (literally "recommended man", a successful examinee at provincial level each year) named Liu had requested to see the treasures. Since the fair was held simply for the imperial envoys to collect jewelries and the common people would not be allowed in. Luckily, this envoy had a high regard for scholars. He not only granted him entrance to the fair but also showed him around the temple to take a look at the treasures.

Amazed by the jewelries, Liu asked the envoy where they came from.

"From places hundreds of miles away."

'But how did they get here?"

"You are a funny guy," the envoy laughed. "The royal court asked for them to come, with the promise of spending a lot of money, and so here they are."

"Those lifeless treasures coming from places hundreds of miles away were of less value than a person," Liu sighed. "No one bothers to spend any money on me." I was wondering which the real treasure is?"

"You believe those jewels are fakes," asked the envoy, oblivious to what Liu meant.

"Your Excellency. These precious stones may be priceless but they are not food when one is hungry and they are not clothes when one is cold so they are of little use to me. I would not consider them real treasures."

"What would you consider the "real" treasures," the envoy asked him with interest.

"Well, Song Dynasty has been invaded and is now in an

unstable situation. To the imperial court, the most valuable "thing" ought to be the people who are willing to fight for the nation and try to help stabilize it. The emperor and his ministers of the monarchy should regard them as treasures and frankly I am one of those patriots," answered Liu hoping to convince the envoy.

The envoy nodded vigorously in response. Liu shared his ideas with him on how to run the country. The envoy quickly appraised the man as an intelligent person with outstanding strategy. He asked Liu why he didn't go to the capital city and showed his talents to the emperor.

"It is difficult for a poor scholar like me to become an official," Liu sighed, "let alone to meet the emperor. And I don't have enough money to get to the capital."

"It may be difficult to become an official but not as difficult to meet the emperor. I can assist you." With that the envoy instructed his assistant to give Liu enough money to get him comfortably to the capital.

"I am indebted to you for your kindness. I will begin my journey to the capital right now," with that he was on his way.

He traveled by boat, but it was slow going. By the time he passed the Five Ridges it was wintertime. It was the longest journey he ever had. As the weather grew colder he fell sick. But he wouldn't let his illness get in the way of his journey. By the time he reached Nan'an in Jiangxi province, it was snowing. The boat tipped when it passed a bridge and he fell into a river. The water was shallow but cold and he was sick and weak. Fortunately an old man riding a donkey happened to pass by. He saw Liu floundering in the water and crying for help. The old man hurried down his donkey, rushed to the riverbank and pulled him ashore. The old man was Chen, the old tutor of Du Liniang. Realizing how sick the young man was, the kindhearted old man persuaded him not to walk any further and convinced him to go take a rest at the nunnery nearby.

"It's called Plum Blossom Nunnery and it's not far from here. I happen to know some medical skills. Why don't you put up for the night in the nunnery? Once you are better you can continue on with your journey."

Liu agreed and thanked the old man for saving his life.

CHAPTER V

It was indeed the same nunnery Du Bao had built it in memory of his decreased daughter. Few people ever visited the site though, except for the old tutor and the Taoist nun who helped run the place together. Liu Mengmei was brought in here, rested under the old man's care for over one month and gradually recuperated.

It was getting warm after a chilly winter. As Liu's strength returned he asked if he could go out for some fresh air.

"There is a garden out back and nobody had ever gone there," the nun told him. "Though it hasn't been tended to for some time there are still flowers. Since you feel so bored, you can go there for a walk. But it feels somewhat sad out there sometimes, so be careful."

"Why sad?" asked Liu.

"Forget it. Just enjoy the walk," the nun sighed. "Go from the gallery, make a turn at the wall with paintings and move on for 30 meters and you will see the hedge gate of the garden."

Sure enough, Liu found the garden following the nun's direction. Pushing open the hedge door, he saw a flowerless garden filled with only ruins and debris. Wild grass was everywhere. The gravel path was covered with mosses. It was early spring, a resurgent season, but the garden showed little signs of life. The nun was right. Something about this deserted garden indeed made Liu depressed and sad.

Walking through the garden he found an exquisite rosewood box by the rockery. He opened it and saw a scroll of painting. As he unfolded it he saw a beautiful lady on the painting. He didn't take any close look at the painting, assuming it was of Mother Buddha. He folded the scroll and carried it back to his room.

Having washed his hands and tidied his clothes, Liu took out the painting from the box, hanged it on the wall and examined it more carefully. After awhile, he noticed that the beauty in the painting did not look much like the Mother Buddha, because she was not sitting on the Lotus Throne as in all the other paintings of her. And it wasn't Chang'e, the Moon Goddess either because she wasn't walking on the auspicious clouds or standing in the Moon Palace with cherry bay surrounding her. This girl in the painting was standing next to a weeping willow. He had no idea who the beauty was.

The more he stared at the picture the more familiar she looked to him. He seemed to have seen her but could not remember where. Soon after ward, he noticed the poem on the painting about the willow and plum. He read the poem several times and confused how much it reminded him of himself. Liu could not take his eyes off the girl who seemed to smile toward him. Her gaze was soft, soulful and sad. He thought for awhile, picked up the brush pen and wrote a poem next to the girl in the picture. He signed his name when he finished. He recalled a story he'd once read about a young scholar who fell in love with a beautiful woman in the painting. His love was so strong that she walked out of the painting and married him. Staring at the portrait in front of him, Liu wished the story wasn't a fairytale and that he too could draw the girl from out of the painting, just like that young scholar in the story. From then on, he would be infatuated by the woman in the painting every evening and called "my beauty, my sister", as if he wanted to make her alive. He barely expected that his evocation would ever work.

As it happened, Liniang's sprite – like all others – had stood before the judge of the netherworld. But when he checked the Register of Judgment he learned that she was not supposed to die so young, and that she would be resurrected after three years passed. The judge sent her to the City of Wrong Death where her

sprite was allowed to wander freely.

Three years passed quickly. Miss Du missed the place she used to live when she was young so much that she "flied" with the night wind to Nan'an and revisited the garden where she had the dream. Each visit made her sadder as the garden grew more desolate. One night towards the end of her three years, she returned to the garden and looked upon the Plum Nunnery in the moonlight. It made her remember her aged father, loving mother and the maid who had been like a sister to her.

The air carried a whisper to her, as if someone was reading a poem. She heard someone calling "Sister, Sister" and chanting a poem. She listened carefully and realized that it was her poem in the painting she had wrote besides her portrait before her death. Knowing that the painting had been hidden in the garden's rockery, she was quite confused. How could anyone chant my poem?

Looking around, she noticed a light coming from the window of a small room in the west veranda of the nunnery. She made her way to the window, looked inside and saw a young scholar censing and worshipping in front of a painting on the wall.

"My beauty, my sister," he repeated quietly.

Without thought, she pushed open the door to the tiny room. A gust of wind entered the room so strongly it nearly blew out the candle. The young man hurriedly put his hands on the painting for fear that the wind might blow the painting away. By the dim candlelight she realized that he was the young scholar in her dream, and that the painting was in fact the one she had painted herself. She also noticed that another poem was now written besides her own and it was signed "Liu Mengmei." "The young man in my dream was holding a willow branch in his hand," Miss Du thought, "so I guess that my future husband would be

surnamed Liu (a homophone to the Chinese word willow). It looks likely that we are connected and it may be a predestined marriage bestowed by the God Heaven." Though exulted, she did not disturb the young scholar. Instead, she changed into a light breeze and drifted away.

She returned to this window day after day to watch him praying in front of her painting. She was so deeply moved by her devotion that she was no longer concerned with all the rules from her life and social etiquette of the young women from respectable families. Nor did she care that he was human while she was a sprite. All she wanted was to return to her human self and live a long life with her lover.

One night as Liu sat before the painting like usual he heard a rustling of the bamboo leaves outside. He listened more closely, and soon heard a knock on his window.

"Who could this be, as it is so late," he asked himself, assuming that it was the nun bringing him tea.

"Is that Mother Stone? Thank you but no tea, please."

"I am not Mother Stone," said a woman outside the window. Puzzled, Liu opened the door hesitantly, only to see a beautiful woman standing before him. With a quick smile she skipped into the room. Confused, he quickly shut the door behind him, afraid that someone might have seen their brief interaction. The woman bashfully greeted the young man. He returned her greeting and asked her which family she came from and why she came here in the dead of night.

"Take a guess, my scholar."

"Are you a fairy descending from heaven?" "How can it be?"

"Maybe you were traveling and got lost? Or you are a runaway?"

"No," she said with a shake of her head and a smile. "Have

you ever dreamed of a lover in this very garden?"

"Yes..."

"I'm here because of those dreams." "Then, where's your home?"

"Not far from here. In the village, near the nunnery, but no one lives there except for my lonely and helpless parents."

"Then why are you here," he asked her, still feeling very confused.

"Because I found you an elegant, handsome, refined young man and I wanted to talk to you."

"Is this a dream?" Liu couldn't place her but he felt as if he had seen her somewhere before. He rubbed his eyes, checking to see if he was dreaming.

"This is not a dream. This is real," the girl answered. "What's your name?"

"You will know everything soon," she wanted to tell him everything but because she still belonged to the sprite world she was afraid she would scare him if she revealed the truth.

"Be patient."

"Fine," he replied slowly. "I will not ask again if you agree to visit me every night."

Died of depression and grieve because of love, the girl had finally met her dream sweetheart and could live happily together. Though a sprite, she felt happier now than when she was a human because she could do whatever she wanted.

CHAPTER VI

Liniang's sprite returned nightly to Liu and before long they had fallen madly in love with one another. Every night he would tidy up the room, light the candles and wait for the lady to come at nightfall. As it got dark, she would show up on time. The two would meet like this every night and two months have passed before anyone had ever noticed.

He knew nothing about her, not even her name, but as time passed he knew he wanted to spend the rest of his life with her. He started preparing himself to ask her for her story so that he could properly propose to her. But she continued to avoid telling him the truth. Still afraid that he would fall out of love with her if he knew what she really was. Her confidence began to fade, not knowing what to do next.

One night, under the tranquil candlelight, it began like all the other nights since they met, the young man mustered up the courage to express his love to her and ask her more about herself.

"You really are not married to anyone?"

"No. I have told you many times I am not. How many more times will I say before you believe me," the girl grumbled bashfully.

"It is not that I don't believe you," he answered quickly. "I just wonder how a girl as beautiful and smart as you hasn't been married off yet."

"I never wanted money or power," she relied. "I just want to marry someone who is smart and who loves me for who I am."

"I love you for who you are." "I know."

"Then, could you marry me?"

"You live so far away from here, how do I know you are not married?"

"I have never been."

"Why don't you visit a matchmaker to find a wife?"

"Lady, I don't even know your name. Why won't you tell me? You could be daughter of the emperor, one from an extraordinary family, a fairy or even a sprite." The pair sat in silence for some time.

The young lady meditated for awhile and said, "Young man, it is not a hard thing to me to tell you my name and marry you because I like you and want to live with you forever. However, as the old saying goes a concubine runs away with her lover while a wife needs to engage with her husband. Before I tell you everything I need to know I can trust you. If we married now in private what would stop you from leaving me later?"

The young man stood up and lit a stick of incense, and then took Liniang's hand and together they knelt in prayer.

"I want to marry this woman and live the rest of my years with her," he looked into her eyes. "I will be damned if I ever deceive you." Liniang was deeply moved to tears by the young man's true affection.

"Why are you crying?"

"I was so moved by your words. Now I want to tell you the truth. But I'm worried it will scare you away," she paused. "First, where did you get the painting?"

"I found it between the rock crevices in the garden one day." "Compare the girl in the painting to me. Which one of the two looks more beautiful?"

Liu slowly compared the painting to the girl sitting before him. He was shocked to find they are identical.

"You two look exactly the same." "It's because the painting is of me."

He looked at the young lady again and excitedly gave the picture a solute. "So God may have been moved by my sincerity and sent you down to my side." He urged the young lady to tell

him more about her.

"My name is Liniang. I am 16 – old enough to get married." "Now I know your name, my sweetheart."

"There's something you don't know, mister. I am not a human, I'm a ghost."

"What do you mean you are a ghost?" "I mean just that. I am a ghost."

The young man was so shocked that he almost fell over his chair. He quickly recovered.

"Now that we are to get married, I have nothing to be afraid of. Even if you are a ghost, I am not leaving you."

"Thank you for your affection. I am a ghost to be resurrected, so I can still be your human wife. Though my body has been buried for three years, it hasn't decayed. Once you open the grave, my spirit and body will be reunited and I will be alive again."

With these words she left, floating on the air.

The next day, the young man went to see the nun. He told her everything about the young lady, her visit and what she had told him about digging up her grave. The nun stared at him in shock, finding the story unbelievable. However, the nun knew that the young man had never met the young lady in life and the girl he had just described could only be the young mistress. She was dubious about what she was told. Finally, she let herself convinced to open up the grave and check.

The two of them walked out to the plum tree by the rockery in the garden. The young man bowed to the tree and then started digging. Before long he dug out the coffin but the rusty coffin nails lining it made him question everything all over again. Could someone really come back to life? What if the coffin is opened and only a skeleton is seen? He was having second thoughts, afraid that a skeleton would greet him upon opening the lid.

A tiny groan came from inside the coffin, interrupting his thoughts. The young man was shocked but delightfully so. Hurriedly, he pulled back the lid and saw a neatly dressed beauty lying inside with her cheeks rosy as if she was sleeping. That was the girl he had been visiting nightly for months now. Her body was warm to the touch. When he hurriedly helped her sit up, the young lady opened her eyes. The nun jumped back in utter disbelief at the scene happening before her eyes. Soon, the nun recovered her senses enough to help. Working together the two of them escorted the lady inside the nunnery.

Liniang grew stronger with each passing day. But every time the young man brought up the subject of marriage she found a way to avoid talking about it. One day, as they were talking about it again in the nun's room, someone knocked on the door. The girl jumped up and hid before the young man had even opened the door. It was Mr. Chen, the old tutor who came to see if the young man would accompany him to the girl's grave the following day in order to pay respect. Liu agreed quickly just to get Chen to leave. When the door was securely shut Liniang reappeared, but her face had lost all color.

"He wants to visit my grave tomorrow! When he gets there, he will find out it has been dug up. At that moment, the girl will be damned as a demon of some sort and you, will be charged with grave digging! What can we do? They thought in silence for what seemed like hours before Liu finally spoke.

"I have an idea. I was en route to Lin'an to take the imperial examination. Why don't we get married tonight and then we leave tomorrow. That way even if the old man discovers the open grave there will be nothing he can do about it."

Left with no other option, the young lady agreed. A few hours later they held a tiny ceremony, with the nun acting as the chief witness. After the ceremony, the newlyweds and the nun fled from the nunnery under the moonlight on the very night on their way to the Lin'an city.

They arrived safe and sound after two days of travel and quickly found an inn to stay in. But the innkeeper informed Liu that the examination had already started. Astonished, the young man rushed to the exam center only to find the doors were closed. He was beside himself, realizing that he had missed his chance to take the exam for another three years.

Luckily for Liu, The Claims Examiner was Miao -the very same envoy of the emperor who had given him money to travel here many months before. Miao, who was overseeing the test, heard someone wailing outside and sent someone out to bring him the noisemaker. He was shocked to see Liu in here. He broke the rules and allowed him to come in and take the exam. Liu thanked Miao and began the test. When the time was up, Miao read Liu's paper several times and found that Liu was indeed very talented and incredibly smart. He hoped that he would take the first place as he arranged the papers and left to report back to the emperor the results.

The day after the trio left the nunnery, the Old Chen discovered the place was empty and deserted. Confused, he walked out to the girl's grave alone only to find it dug up and the coffin completely uncovered. Chen decided that it had to be Liu, who, obsessed with money, must have lost his mind and robbed the grave. The old man was so angry that his goatee trembled.

"How dare you," he yelled to the empty garden. "I saved your life and this is how you repay my kindness? You are a heartless and ungrateful bastard."

The old man was heartbroken for the poor girl who couldn't find peace even in her death. Her father entrusted him and the

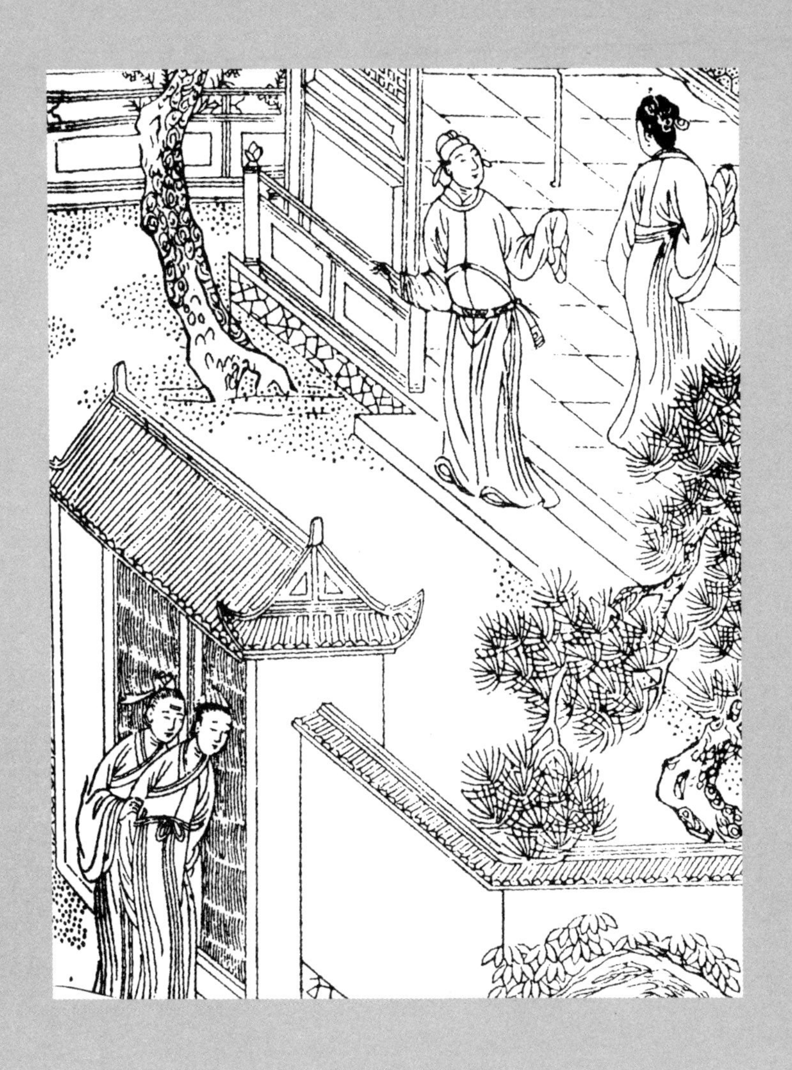

nun with protecting her grave, and he had failed the simplest of tasks. He stood weeping next to the empty grave before realizing that he needed to inform the Lord about what had happened. He hurried inside, packed his bag and left for Huaian where the girl's parents now lived.

CHAPTER VII

During this time in Huaian, a warning was sounded as the Jin army had invaded the country and the frontier was in peril. The emperor frantically summoned his civilian officials and army generals to discuss the war situation. The local magistrates were ordered to fight back the invaders. Announcement of the examination result was temporarily postponed because of the pending war. The lord quickly sent his wife and her maid to the capital for refuge and then led his army to the frontier to fight.

By now the emperor of the Jin Dynasty (AD 1115-1234) had successfully concurred over half of Song's territory and he wanted more. Hangzhou was known for being a beautiful city in this region and the Jin emperor wanted it to be his land. When he heard about a Haoshan Hill in the city, he asked someone to draw a picture of the hill, the West Lake and himself riding a horse with a whip in hand. The painting was inscribed words as On Horse at the First Peak of Haoshan Hill. Jin Emperor would dream to take over Hangzhou city. However, things did not go the way as he wished. After his initial attempt to march directly into the city limits failed, he decided that the best way to take over Hangzhou was to surround the city and penetrate it from all sides. He recruited local thieves and robbers to his ever-growing army, and promoted his man, Li—a boorish and short-tempered fighter—to be the commander-in-chief. Li was instructed to enlist his own men and work at harassing the Song border.

Li had guts and muscle but no brains for war tactics. Therefore, the real commander-in-chief was not him but his wife, an extraordinary woman who excelled in marksmanship, knew military strategy and tactics well and was very resourceful. When Du became the magistrate, he had been busy building defense works and storing food, making the city securely guarded as tight as a metal pail. Li was growing more and more anxious over his failing efforts to break the defense of Hangzhou city. His wife suggested to him that he attack the providence of Huaian in order to lure Du's reinforcement army away from the city. Then, the men who stayed behind could have an easier entrance into the city and gave them the upper hand. Li agreed that this was a great idea and soon ordered his 30,000 troops to tightly encircle Huaian.

The attack on Huaian frightened the Song emperor and his ministers. Unaware that this was a plot to leave Hangzhou unguarded the emperor ordered Du to take his men and defeat the rebels at Huaian. Du, taking his wife with him, quickly followed the emperor's order, departing for Huaian with his army by boat.

As they were 50 kilometers away, a bad news reached them that Huaian city was in a desperate situation. The boats were slow. Du was worried that they wouldn't be able to reach the city in time so he changed route and switched to a land attack. The soldiers had to travel by horseback but Du's wife was not a horse rider and therefore had to take a sedan chair, which is much slower than boats. This greatly slowed down the army. For this reason, the magistrate had no other options but decided that his wife and her servant girl go to Lin'an instead to take temporary refuge. The couple parted each other.

Exhausted as they were, Du and his men marched on for the rest of the day and night without stop. By dawn they had reached the besieged Huaian city. At the first sight of the aggressive and threatening invaders Du ordered his soldiers to break the siege and meanwhile sent an urgent request for reinforcement from the neighboring Lin'an city.

Noticing Du's approaching army, Li sent his men to fend off the attack. Since Li's real objective was to take over the beautiful Yangzhou city, he only used one thousand of his soldiers to meet

enemy attack. It was a fierce fight and Du successfully broke the siege and dashed into the city. Li was not worried too much. Instead, he encircled the city once again and waited until Du surrendered because of the lack of provisions. Once inside the city, Du found it guarded by a troop of 13,000 soldiers with stocks that could survive the siege for at least 6 months. Only both the civil officials and generals were so scared of death, they thought about fleeing the city more than defending it. The first thing first was the stability, reorganization of troop and defense preparation.

The war not only shocked the emperor and his ministers but also affected life of the populace, the common people like the gentle and frail scholar Liu Mengmei. After the exam had ended he ran back to the inn where he, Liniang and the nun had taken up lodging. He quickly told them about the war and postponement of the announcements of the exam results.

"It really doesn't matter. The results will be released eventually," Liniang was distracted. "My father is the magistrate of Hangzhou. I'm worried about my parents. What if they're in trouble," she fought back tears. "Liu, it may take some more days to get the exam results, could you go and find out if they are ok?"

"Of course!"

"I only worry about leaving you alone."

"Don't worry. I have Mother Stone to stay with me."

"You're sure? Alright then. Do you want me to tell your parents about your resurrection when I find them?"

"Yes, they might not believe you though. It is unacceptable for an old-fashioned and conservative person like my father. Du Liniang thought for a moment and told Liu, "You could bring the painting with you and used it to explain that we were destined by heaven to be together. Tell him that you took sanctuary at the nunnery, stumbled upon my grave on day, the ground caved in and I was brought back." Liu shook his head, hoping this would work. He readied himself to leave, knowing there was no other option. "Promise me you'll be careful? I'll miss you."

"I am afraid no one would believe your story. I'd better tell it as it is and say you just came into my room and dated me."

The girl flushed and said, "Stop kidding any more. Let me help you pack. You take care of yourself on the road. I'll miss you a lot."

At that, Liu bid farewell to his wife and set out for Huaian.

CHAPTER VIII

After Chen Zuiliang , the old pedant, discovered the excavation of the grave, he took it as a serious matter and thought he must report to his former master immediately. He rushed to Yangzhou where the Lord once stayed only to find that he had been reassigned to guard Huaian city. In spite of the tiredness from his trip, he was on his way to Huaian again. However, something that he never dreamt of happened. He was caught by the enemy soldier at Huaian before he went into the city.

Li and Du had been fighting over Huaian for over a month at this point, though neither one seemed to be gaining much ground. The city was defended so securely that Li was not able to break it. Li was a man of quick temper and he didn't know what to do next when his people caught Chen. He was ecstatic to learn that the old man used to be a hanger-on of Du's family. He wanted to use this leverage the best he could but he was unsure of how to best go about doing so. Like before, his wife had a plan.

"You have killed many people since this war began, including old women and children. We could get two heads and say that they are of Du's wife and her servant girl. Let the old pedant bring the news to Du in the city. Du will be so distraught and his people so panic that they won't be able to defend the city. Then, we can attack."

As they discussed, Li had the old man untied just as one of his men entered the room carrying with him two human heads.

"Our soldiers have killed Magistrate Du's family on their way to Yangzhou and chopped off their heads for reward."

"How do I know that they are real? Can't our soldiers mistake them? Can't those heads be fakes," Li questioned.

"They are absolutely real. This head belongs to the magistrate's wife. That one belongs to her servant girl."

The old man moved closer. He started to fluster at the soldier's words. He was dim-sighted from old age and scared to death at the sight of these two bloody human heads. He truly believed that he was looking at Mrs. Du and her servant girl's heads. He could not help but cried.

"Oh my god it's true! How could this have happened? What am I going to do?"

"You are a stupid old man. What are you howling for? It's nothing that Du's wife and her servant girl have been killed! I am going to sweep into the city and kill Du himself."

"Please have a heart and spare my Lord." The old man was so scared he shivered convulsively as he pleaded for his boss' life.

"Spare him? It's not that easy. The only way I could allow him to live is for him to hand over the city. Otherwise, he will end up just like his wife."

"Please. Let me go into the city and talk to my lord. I promise to report back to you once I have any news."

Li, happy that every thing was going according to plan, released the old man who ran off in search of Du. After a short period of frantic searching he finally located the magistrate who was surprised that he would meet the old man in here. With no time for pleasantries he launched directly into his story, tears in eyes.

"My Lord, your wife was killed by the enemy soldiers on their way to seek asylum."

"How could it be? How did you know?"

The Old Chen told Du what he saw and heard at the enemy camp and asserted emphatically that the heads were that of Mrs. Du and her servant girl. His sobbing grew uncontrollably making it nearly impossible for the old man to speak. Du was so heartbroken he wailed loudly. The officials beside their chief couldn't help but shed tears. As the official appointed by the court, Du quickly collected his faculties and calmed down, aware that this was no time to show weakness. He wiped his tears away and reprimanded the local officials. "What did you cry for? My wife was appointed by the court and she died a glorious death. I will never lose my head over this. The soldiers' morale is more important." Du then asked the old pedant, "This culprit will not leave the matter at that. What else did they say to you?"

"They also wanted to kill you," the old pedant stuttered. He moved closer and whispered to the magistrate's ear and said, "But it's not you that Li really wanted. It's the city. It's detrimental to everyone if this war stays at a stalemate. I think you should let them take the city and stop killing one another's troops off."

"What! It's ridiculous! I am shocked to hear that as a learned scholar you would even have the gall to suggest such a thing. Only because of your connection to my daughter will I not punish you for that," he shook his head angrily.

"How many seats were there in the tent when you were there, one or two," Du asked Chen.

"Two. Li and his wife sat side by side."

Du shook his head, obviously worried about something, but Chen couldn't figure out what. He was about to ask when Du turned back to him.

"Chen, what brought you here in the first place? You must have already been headed here when you captured.

The old man was puzzled, not knowing what he meant. He was about to ask the magistrate when something seemed to have occurred to him.

"Mr. Chen, why did you come here in such turmoil?"

"I was so sad about the death of your wife and her servant girl and so overwhelmed by everything that has happened since I got here that I nearly forgot what I came here for. I needed to tell you that your daughter's grave was robbed, and her body taken."

"What! My daughter's grave was robbed! My poor daughter! For three years, who could have any desire to ... do such a terrible thing?"

"Some time after you left a young scholar arrived at the nunnery. He was quite ill at the time and so we told him to stay there until he regained his health. He had never shown any signs of interest, but then a few weeks ago when I found that the grave was dug up and robbed, the remain of your daughter was gone and the young guy, too. It must be him who committed this crime at the sight of money by excavating the grave at night and ran away. Now the grave was robbed and even the remains disappeared. I would guess that the young guy threw the skeleton into the pond. What a sinful thing he did!"

"My family was haunted by misfortunes," the magistrate sighed. "First, my daughter's grave was robbed and then my wife was killed. As the old saying goes, 'One can barely live for 100 years and after he dies his grave can barely be kept intact for 100 years.' No dead resurrects. What's done is done. There's nothing we can do about it. Let's submit it to the will of Heaven. I truly appreciate your traveling so far to give me this message, Chen."

"Thank you for your trust. This is part of my job. Please let me know if anything else I could do for you," he paused. "I've grown hopeless in the last few years, there are things I want but I have no way of achieving them."

"I do have something you could do for me. I left in such a hurry that there are things left unfinished. I have written two letters for Li and his wife in which I ask him to dissolve his army and pledge allegiance to Song—I want you to deliver the letters to him. If you can persuade and make him surrender it will not go unnoticed. I will inform the emperor and you will be given an official post."

"I am ready to offer this ser vice." At that Chen took the letters from Du and set off towards Li's camp.

Although Jin emperor named Li one of his seigniors, he only took him as a dog and never completely trusted him. The emperor would send emissaries to check him out. Those emissaries were insolent and rude to Li and they would only extort wealth. Some of them even took liberty of Li's wife. Li was not happy and sometimes mad about all these, but he never thought about breaking away from Jin Dynasty. His wife however had long had the idea of leaving Jin. Now, Li stationed his troops outside Huaian city. There was no way for him to break the defense so he had nothing to report to emperor about his mission. The emperor repeatedly urged him to attack. Li was in a dilemma. Du, his adversary, knew this every well, so he decided to take this opportunity to drive a wedge between Li and the dynasty he worked for. Du wanted to make him surrender and give allegiance to Song Dynasty.

When Chen returned, Li invited him into his tent desperate for some good news that Du would gave him the city.

"So is Du handing his city over to me?"

"A city doesn't mean much. I am here to offer you the position of a king."

"But I am already a king," replied Li.

"Then think of this offer as a promotion. Du asked me to give you this letter," he handed over the letters to Li and his wife. The letter reads:

The Jin people are cruel and backstabbing. They cannot be trusted to maintain a long-term relationship with. If you would consider joining me and pledge allegiance to Song, I can guarantee a higher position for you as well as great wealth. I will personally ask the Emperor to let you keep your current title and give you wife on as well.

The letter hit a nerve with Li. He and his wife began discussing the new option immediately. Li agreed with his wife to leave Jin Dynasty and raise siege of Huaian city. This offer seemed to be very attractive to Li. Mesmerized by the letters, he really wanted to pledge allegiance to Song after he withdrew his troops, thinking he would be given a higher rank. However, his wife was smarter and more skeptical.

"The titles conferred upon by the emperor are unreal. I'd bet that once you surrender he'd have you killed before the day ends. I don't think we should work for either emperor. Why don't we just leave all of this and become pirates. That way we'll live under no one's rule but our own."

Li thought it over, but before long decided that his wife had a point. He disbanded his army and left the city by boat.

CHAPTER IX

After the young scholar left, Du Liniang lived with the nun in a rented house outside the Huaian city. One evening, as they were chatting by the oil lamp, it became dimmer and the room darker. The lamp was burning out of oil. As soon as the nun left the room to get more oil there was a knock on the door. She opened the door and saw an old woman and a girl standing before her. They told her that they'd been traveling for days, exhausted and asked if they could put up for one night in here. Du Liniang ushered them inside the dimly-lit room, making eye contact with the woman. In the darkness it was more difficult to make out one another's feathers but slowly recognition spread over both faces. Liniang stood face to face with her mother and her servant girl.

"Chunxiang, Take a close look at the girl and tell me who she likes like."

"I may be wrong but she looks like your daughter," the servant replied timidly.

"Look around and see if anyone else is in the room. If not, then we may have encountered a ghost," said the old lady who was limp and flaccid by now.

At this moment, Du Liniang has recognized her mother and servant girl. However, she never thought they should have appeared at this wild and desolate place outside town. She didn't know what had happened.

"What are you doing here?" Liniang was shocked that her mother and Chunxiang were traveling so far from the city walls.

"Where did you come from?"

"We're running from Huaian where my husband is the magistrate but it is not safe there right now."

This confirmed everything for Liniang and she threw herself into her mother's arms and began crying. But the mother was so confused and slightly frightened by the image of her daughter standing before her.

"How is this possible? Are you really human again? Are you real?"

"Don't be afraid, mom. I am flesh and blood," Liniang reached out and took her mother's hand in her own. The mother shook with fear and grabbed onto Chunxiang. She wanted to flee but her feet were so weak to move. She could do nothing but implored repeatedly. Just then the nun returned with the lamp oil, literally lighting up the room. Chunxiang had sharp eyes and she recognized her.

"Madam. Didn't you see this is Mother Stone, the same nun you and your husband left in charge of our old home?"

"Mother Stone. Please come over. Look, by chance my mother found her way here but she believed I am a ghost," said the daughter, clutching the nun's hand and asking her to testify her identity.

The nun refilled the oil in the lamp to make the room brighter. Afterward, she started to comfort the mother. The four women had a long and slightly confusing talk. Liniang told the story of her resurrection but left out the part about her going to the nunnery dating Liu, the young scholar. She told her mother that the God from Mount Tai appeared in Liu's dream and asked him to dig up my grave and make me resurrected. Mrs. Du had a hard time believing that the girl sitting before her was indeed her daughter but she eventually calmed down and took Liniang in her arms. The mother and daughter finally recognized each other.

Needless to say, this is a happy reunion of mother and daughter. However, the young scholar still searching for his father-in-law was not as lucky. The couple did not have much money in the first place. When they left Nan'an with the nun, they spent on the jewelry buried in the grave on the way. Before he left home, the girl gave him some of her jewelry buried with her in the grave. The jewelry was worth some money but the young man had no idea of their worth and value. Not even the worldly wisdom. He was always ripped off when he tried to exchange money with the jewelry. Soon, he ran out of money and by the time he reached Huaian he was penniless. It was getting dark and he felt exhausted. He stumbled into a lodge looking for a place to sleep for the night.

The innkeeper looked Liu up and down. He hadn't showered in days, had the painting stuck out from his backpack, and he carried a broken umbrella. Fearing that the guy couldn't afford the lodging, he insisted that he paid for the room up front. Liu debated trading things in his bag, a brush pen and two books, for a room. He didn't want to exchange them, especially to a man who had no interest in their worth. So he handed over his umbrella hoping it would be enough to cover a night of lodging and a small meal.

The inn-keeper looked at him contemptuously and asked, "What if it rains?"

"It doesn't matter anymore. This is my destination." "So you plan to starve to death here?"

"Any chance you know Mr. Du, the magistrate," he asked, ignoring the innkeeper's comment.

"Of course. Who doesn't? He is hosting a banquet for the officials in the city tomorrow night."

"I am his son-in-law."

At this the inn-keeper laughed out loud. His eyes were surveying Liu for a second time. But Liu held a straight face and stood his ground.

"So you are the son-in-law of Mr. Du. Luckily you mentioned this. Come over quickly and read the bulletin written by your father-in-law." The innkeeper dragged him to the wall and pointed to a piece of paper on it.

Beware of fraud. My estate was robbed and there may be a man going around claiming to be my relation. I have no sons or nephews, and my only daughter never married. Arrest this man if you find him.

The bulletin was signed with a scarlet stamp.

"Now you read it with your own eyes. There's nothing more you can say. If you leave now, I won't call the police."

He was driven out of the inn. Hungry and penniless, he was a complete stranger to this city. In his desperation he couldn't help but cry. It was dark by now, and he was so tired all he could do was huddle underneath the eaves of nearby house and wait for morning to come.

With the rising sun, Liu was up and hurrying towards the magistrate's office. There were dozens of people coming and going from the building that was decorated with lanterns and streamers in preparation for the banquet the innkeeper had mentioned. The dinner was to celebrate the withdrawal of the enemy troops. The government officials and despotic gentry were all dressed up for the occasion. He managed to get to the gate of the building. He told the guard his story, in hopes it would get him inside. The gatekeeper could hardly believe that this shabby looking guy was the son-in-law of the magistrate. They thought he was just kidding. The gatekeeper was not willing to waste any of his time.

"All the officials are just inside and everyone is busy. Why don't you wait outside for awhile?"

Liu nodded at the guard and sat on the steps, waiting. "It was noisy outside," he thought. "When everyone got in, it was a mess inside. My father-in-law must be busy entertaining his guests. OK, I wait." It was about noontime and he was growing hungrier.

The gatekeeper still refused to let him inside. Liu kept begging him to inform the people inside of his coming. Seeing that the guy lingered around and was reluctant to leave, the gate keeper began to worry that maybe he was in fact telling the truth and was indeed the son-in-law of the magistrate. "The high ranking officials may have poor relatives," he thought. "What by any chance if this priggish pedant had any relation with the magistrate and he blamed, then it would be too much for me to take on." Suddenly fearing for his job he quickly rushed inside and reported Liu's presence to his boss. At this, he quickly went in and reported to his boss.

The magistrate just received an imperial edict transferring him to the capital where he became Prime Minister for his effort to end the war. He was walking among his officials when the gatekeeper rushed up to him and reported that his son-in-law was waiting outside.

"I don't have any son-in-law!" he shouted. "Have you not noticed the bulletins I've sent all over town? How can you bother me with this? Needless to say, this guy is a swindler. Get rid of him!"

The gatekeeper felt stupid for his mistake. He returned to his post, grabbed Liu and dragged him out of the courtyard without a word. Liu began screaming at the guard and a loud argument soon broke out. Liu broke out of the guard' grip and ran inside the building. Chaos erupted. The guard and servants chased after him. Du, who was trying to celebrate, grew quickly annoyed by the noise.

"Who the hell is this man? Catch him and send him to Lin'an. I will deal with him after I arrive in the capital."

After so many hardships, Liu finally arrived at Huaian. But he never expected his father-in-law would have him arrested. He hardly had any place to vent his grievances.

CHAPTER X

Du Bao had received his promotion for ending the war. The emperor also kept Du's promise and made Chen one of his official messengers. Chen would be responsible for delivering the emperor's orders and edicts. The old man was beyond happy with this title, he felt rejuvenated and more confident than he had in years.

As the soldiers dispersed the nation gradually returned to normal. The supervisor of the exams finally requested that the emperor read over the results and name the top scholar of the year. Liu was, of course, one of the successful candidates. It was a Song Dynasty tradition that a celebratory banquet be thrown for all the exam candidates. The dinner was held in the royal garden, Qionglin Garden, and hence became known as the Qionglin Feast.

Chen was instructed to invite all the candidates. As he was going over the list of names he discovered that the top-ranked scholar of the year was Liu. Though Chen was still angry with Liu for digging up the grave, he was clear that Liu was the most successful candidate who deserved the opportunity to dine with the emperor.

As the one who was responsible for tracking down each of the scholars, Chen searched high and low for Liu. The scouts were sent out but everyone came back empty-handed. Chen wanted to make a good impression with his first official task as messenger so he sent out even more people to locate Liu.

What Chen didn't know was that Liu had actually been arrested by his unsuspecting father-in-law, and was now locked up in the capital's prison. Du had nearly forgotten about the young man he'd had arrested. But after a few days he remembered and sent for Liu so that he could question him.

Unlike the other prisoners, Liu did not go down on his knees begging for mercy. Instead, he stood upright in front of the court insisting that he was in fact Du's son-in-law. But his insistence only angered Du more.

"My daughter has been dead for three years and she was never married! She wasn't even engaged when she passed. What is this nonsense about you being my son-in-law all about? Did you honestly think you could claim a government job using such a flimsy story?"

"I know I look miserable and shabby right now," laughed Liu. "But I'm smart, and with my skills I don't worry about food and clothes. In fact, I could pass the imperial exam. Why would I pretend to be your son-in-law?"

"So this is how you chose to play your hand? Fine," Du said calmly. "Search his bag for stolen goods."

The guards searched Liu's single bag and discovered the painting. But Liu didn't panic. He believed that when Du saw Liniang's self-portrait he would be allowed to speak and soon be acknowledged as family. However, the painting only reminded Du of his daughter's grave robbery.

"What's your name?"

"Liu Mengmei from Ling'an." "Have you ever been to Nan'an?"

"Yes. In fact I stayed there for some time."

"Did you know Mother Stone, the Nun and Chen, the Tutor?"

"Yes, I know both of them."

"So you are the grave robber," Du laughed humorlessly. "I've been looking for you. Didn't expect you would surrender yourself, though. Not only did you rob my daughter's grave but you pretended to be a relation of mine," Du shook his head in disgust. "Hang him up and whip him."

Liu was hung up and whipped before he had a chance to explain himself. The people of the city overheard Liu's cries and couldn't stop themselves from looking into the court to see what all the noise was about. One such passerby was an old man with a hunchback, who had once been a servant in Liu's home in Ling'nan. It had been years since he had seen Liu, but he had no family of his own and hence thought of Liu as his family. The old man had in fact been searching for Liu, and knew that he had journeyed to the capital to take the palace exam.

Among others who passed by while Liu was being whipped were several errand goers hoping to hear who had been named the top-ranked scholar in the nation. The hunchbacked old man heard them say Liu's name, and spoke up.

"Has the list been posted yet? Has the Top Scholar been announced yet?"

"Liu Mengmei was named as the Top Scholar for this year," answered one of the errand goers. "We are under orders to find him."

The old man was relieved to hear that his young master had received the grand title. He informed the trio of errand goers that the man they were looking for was, in fact, the one whose screams had distracted them. The trio of Chen's men went inside the court, and soon confirmed that the man being whipped was indeed Liu Mengmei.

Word was sent back to Chen that they had located the Top Scholar of the Year, and also that he had been beaten. But it was more than Chen alone was capable of dealing with so he sought a meeting with the court's claims examiner.

Liu instantly recognized the claims examiner and knew that he'd probably be all right. Seeing Chen, as the royal messenger, however, took him by surprise. He greeted the old hunchback and then sent him to fetch his wife and the nun as quickly as possible. But the old man deducted from their brief conversation that Liu had not robbed the girl's grave, and that she had been resurrected.

The claims examiner requested that Du release Liu. Du was informed that the emperor had named Liu the Top Scholar for that year. Du couldn't believe the news. He insisted that there must have been some mistake made.

"Prime minister, I personally gave him money to cover his traveling expenses when he was on his way to take the imperial exam. I was also the supervisor for the test. No mistake has been made."

Du knew that the claims examiner was telling the truth so he had no other choice but to listen. He ordered Liu to be untied and told him he could attend the feast, but he was still reluctant to trust the scholar. It was greatly confusing for him, how such a horrible human could also be the year's top-ranked scholar. Du was storming around the room, trying to ease some of his anger, when Chen arrived.

"Congratulations, my lord!" Chen said with a bow.

"For what?"

"You've been promoted to Prime Minister, you're daughter has been resurrected and you will soon be reunited with her, and lastly, that your son-in-law has been names the top-scholar of the nation. Aren't those things worth celebrating?"

"Mr. Chen, what are you talking about?" Du, who knew nothing about his daughter's resurrection, was completely taken aback by Chen's words.

"Do you expect me to believe that this man is my son-in-low? "And what are you implying about my daughter? Wasn't it you who recently informed me of her robbed grave? How could you say such nonsense to me?"

"Everything I've said is true. Your daughter—human or not—is alive, I believe."

"You are mistaken, Mr. Chen. I refuse to believe this mumbo jumbo. There is no such thing as resurrection. As the prime minister—if you really heard this story—I must report it to the emperor. As royal messenger, please relay this information to him immediately."

CHAPTER XI

Following Liu's instructions, the old servant left to fetch Liniang and the nun. Upon his arrival he informed them of all that had taken place, and that Liu had been named the nation's top scholar of the year. Liniang was beside herself with happiness as this news followed her reunion with her mothers.

Liniang hurriedly put on her dress and the group soon departed from the house. The city was bustling with activity, so they barely noticed when a stocky soldier approached them. However, he was following the emperor's orders to find Liniang and bring her to court. The emperor, by now, had heard that Liu was both the top scholar and a grave robber, and the rumor that Liniang had been resurrected, so he decided to see for himself in before a final verdict was made.

Liniang and her mother were happy to hear that Du, now prime minister, was alive, and but it upset them that Du believed Liu, his son-in-law, to be a grave robber, and that he wanted him dead. The soldier escorted the group to the audience hall of the emperor's palace

Du and Liu had arrived before Liniang and had quickly begun arguing. Du accused Liu of robbing his daughter's grave, causing Liu to lash out.

"And you are a sinner!" Liu yelled.

"I won the war against the rebels. What made you to call me a sinner?"

"The imperil court didn't know, did they?" questioned Liu with a smile. "You didn't win the war, only half of it, at most."

"What do you mean by 'half'?"

"You didn't defeat the enemy troops. You lonely coaxed the general and his wife to retreat. The work is only half-done."

Du was shaking with rage. He grabbed Liu's collar and shouted in his face. "If you don't stop talking nonsense, I will confront you in the audience hall."

"Who the hell is making so much noise in the imperial court?" demanded Chen, barging into the room. His head turned back and forth between Du and Liu, taking a deep breath he politely asked Du to release his grip on Liu. Angrily, the prime minister pushed Liu away and took a step back.

"What has he done to annoy you so much?" Chen asked Du.

"Besides robbing my daughter's grave?" Du spit out. "He called me a sinner."

"You think you're innocent, but I don't," laughed Liu loudly. "You are guilty of three sins when it comes to your daughter."

"Nonsense! What are they, then?"

"First, when she was alive you kept your daughter isolated from the world. Secondly, after she died you didn't come home but instead had her buried and a private nunnery built. Thirdly, when I told you I was your son-in-law you had me arrested and beaten, because you thought I was poor. Are you not guilty of these things?"

Du was speechless.

"You have a sharp tongue Liu," Chen cut in, attempting to assist Du. "Now that you are a member in the family, why don't you two try to make peace with one another? If nothing else, just for my sake."

"Do I know you?" Liu raised his eyebrows, confused. "You don't recognize me?"

Liu took a step closer to the old messenger. Finally, it dawned on him that this was the same man who had saved him from the river so many months ago. His hand flew to his head in shock.

"Chen! You rescued me from the river that day, and brought me back to the nunnery. But, why did you tell Mr. Du that it was me who robbed the grave of his daughter? You have heard the truth now. As the emperor's messenger, will you please help to correct this mess?"

"Don't worry," Chen laughed, "I will do everything I can to tell the emperor the truth."

Before long the three men were summoned to meet with the emperor. They entered the audience hall and Du's eyes fell on Liniang. But, like her mother, he believed her to be a ghost or some type of evil spirit playing a horrible trick on all of them.

The emperor questioned both Liu and Du about Liniang. Liu approached her happily.

"Your Majesty. This is my wife, Liniang."

"My daughter had been dead for three years," said Du coldly to the emperor. "While this ... thing here looks like her she can't be my daughter. I believe her to be some sort of demon or succubus. My advice would be to kill her or she will soon reveal her true self."

"How can you be so cruel? You are her father!" Liu was disgusted by Du's words, so he turned to the emperor. "Your Majesty, he is wrong, and I believe he feels guilty over his mistreatment of her when she was alive before. He's afraid that her resurrection would ruin his good name, but in fact she did resurrect. And we have been married since then. Please perceive and make a wise judgment, Your Majesty."

The emperor was confused by both their stories, and having never met Liniang before, he had no way of knowing what the truth was.

"Ms. Liniang," he decided. "Why don't you share your story with us all?"

Liniang stepped forward. She told the emperor everything: the dream, her illness, and her death; and then about meeting Liu as a ghost and finally of her resurrection. Liu moved up next to

her and gave his side of the story. By the time they had finished the emperor had been convinced that Liniang had in fact been resurrected and was not a demon or a threat.

Du, too, felt as if they must be telling the truth, but then quickly became upset that she would choose to shame her family by deciding on her own marriage without consulting with him, her mother, or a matchmaker. He informed the emperor that he was unwilling to accept his daughter's marriage and would not accept her back into his family.

"Liu accepted me as a ghost! I have been dead for three years and now—by some miracle—I stand here before my own father and you refuse to recognize me as your child? Fine," she shook her head in a mixture of sadness and disgust. "I have found my mother and she has already claimed me as her daughter."

Mrs. Du and then nun were quickly brought into the audience hall, which sent a great shock through Du who was still under the assumption that the rebels had beheaded her.

"They both must be two evil spirits!" Du told the emperor. "My wife was slain by the rebels in Yangzhou. They must be evil spirits disguised as my wife and daughter to cheat people."

Mrs. Du spoke up quickly with her and Chunxiang's story of how they ran from the city and purely by coincidence and luck arrived at her daughter's doorstep. Chen also decided to step in at this moment and admitted that he hadn't actually checked to see if the heads were indeed those of Mrs. Du and Chunxiang.

"I was too scared and might not think right. At the time I believed the opposing general. But now I realize my mistake. I'm very sorry for the confusion, but this is definitely Mrs. Du."

The emperor, overwhelmed with the story unfolding before him, gave his acceptance of Liniang's resurrection, and ordered Du to accept his daughter and reunite with his wife. He then gave his permission for Liniang and Liu to marry.

It took a while for everything to settle and sink in. Everyone thanked the emperor for his kindness and help, and then left the audience hall in a large group.

"Congratulations on your promotion," Mrs. Du said to her husband taking his hand in her own.

"I thought you were dead," he stopped walking and looked at her. "I didn't think I would see you again." He hugged her.

"Dad," Liniang walked over to her parents, tears in her eyes.

"Stay away from me!" Du demanded, letting go of his wife and reaching his hand towards Chen. "I have heard so many ghost stories these days and I have become suspicious of Liu. Are you sure he is not a ghost?"

"My Lord, you worry too much," Mrs. Du spoke calmly. "It may sound shocking but Liniang is alive. We have her back and our son-in-law has been blessed with a great honor. This is good news, so why are you still suspicious? Liniang is back—I will keep her beside me, even if she is a ghost."

But Du continued to refuse. Liu, who stood by watching all of this, grew angry with his heartless father-in-law. Once again the two men began fighting with one another.

"Du," Chen stepped in. "His Majesty has ordered that you recognize your daughter. If you continue on like this, how do you expect me to report to him?"

"Fine, if my daughter is real I can recognize her, but I will never accept this self-claimed son-in-law. She must severe ties with him."

"I owe this man my life. He has my loyalty. Even if I die again I will not betray him. I spent three years wandering through nothing, now I am alive and happy and you want to force me to die all over again?"

Liniang worked herself into such a state that she passed out on the floor. Her mother dropped down next to her and cried. Liu grabbed Du and began yelling again.

"Stop this! Du, this is only your fault," said Chen. "The emperor gave his order, everyone except you is happy with it. Are you willing to take responsibility for your daughter if something unfortunate happens to her?" Liniang stirred on the ground but did not get up. Liu took a deep breath and decided to try a new approach with Du.

"Please, Mr. Du, Liniang and I love each other. I have treated her only with respect and she has done the same to me. She loves you, too. Please do this for her sake."

"All right," Du consented realizing he had little choice in the matter anyway. "I recognize my daughter." Liniang smiled from the ground.

"What about Liu?" she asked.

"If you are my daughter and the two of you are married he has become my son-in-law," Du finally consented, reluctantly.

And with that life continued. Du remained the prime minister, and Liu grew in a higher rank. Liniang and her husband lived happily ever after. They often traveled back to the Peony Pavilion by the rockery in the garden where they first met.